PROBUDITI!

CHRIS VAN ALLSBURG

Houghton Mifflin Company
Boston 2006

To Donna McCarthy

Copyright © 2006 by Chris Van Allsburg

www.houghtonmifflinbooks.com

Library of Congress Cataloging-in-Publication Data

Van Allsburg, Chris.
Probuditi! / written and illustrated by Chris Van Allsburg.
p. cm.
Summary: On his birthday, Calvin and his friend Rodney see a
magician perform, then copy him by hypnotizing Calvin's little sister,
but the joke is on them when they are unable to snap her out of it.
ISBN-13: 978-0-618-75502-8 (hardcover)
ISBN-10: 0-618-75502-0 (hardcover)
[1. Hypnotism—Fiction. 2. Brothers and sisters—Fiction. 3. Tricks
—Fiction. 4. Birthdays—Fiction.]   I. Title.
PZ7.V266Pro 2006
[E]—dc22
2006007980

Printed in the United States of America
WOZ 10 9 8 7 6 5 4 3 2 1

Calvin waited quietly outside Trudy's bedroom. Then it happened—a scream, a very loud scream. Calvin ran to his room and dived into bed. He heard Mama coming down the hall.

"Did you do this?" Calvin looked out from under the covers. His mother stood over him, holding a rubber spider. "Do what?" he asked. "You put that thing in my bed," Trudy told him, stepping out from behind Mama.

"Don't think just because it's your birthday you can get away with something like this," Mama scolded. "You do want your present, don't you?" That wiped the smile off Calvin's face. "Course I do," he said. "Then you apologize." Calvin dropped his head. "Sorry, Trudy," he muttered.

"Here," Mama said. "Happy birthday." At the breakfast table she handed Calvin an envelope. Inside were tickets to the matinee show of Lomax the Magnificent, the world-famous magician and hypnotist. "You've got two tickets there," Mama said, "and I know somebody who'd really love to go along." She smiled at Trudy.

"You don't mean her, do you?" Calvin asked, eyeing his little sister. "Well, that would be nice. But those tickets are yours. If you want to ask somebody—" Calvin didn't wait for his mother to finish. He bolted out of the house to tell Rodney, his pal next door, that the two of them were going to see Lomax the Magnificent.

"How'd he do that?" Rodney whispered. Calvin shook his head in amazement as he and his friend sat in the darkened theater, watching Lomax slide a burning candle in one ear and pull it out the other. Then the magician invited a woman from the audience onto the stage.

She sat down in front of a spinning spiral disc, staring at it. Lomax leaned over and whispered to her, then spoke loudly: "You are a chicken, madam!" The woman jumped up, strutted around in a circle and flapped her arms, then climbed onto the chair, clucking loudly and bobbing her head up and down. Lomax then snapped his fingers and shouted out, "PROBUDITI!" The woman instantly stopped and looked out at the audience, mystified by their wild laughter. Calvin and Rodney thought it was the funniest thing they had ever seen.

"Spaghetti," said Calvin. "Yeah," answered Rodney, "with meatballs." The boys talked about dinner on the bus ride home, because Mama always cooked whatever her children asked for on their birthdays. Rodney was coming, too. "And we've got to have that chocolate cake your mom makes," he said. "Oh, yeah," said Calvin, "we definitely will be having some of that."

"All right then," Mama said, "spaghetti it is." The cake had just come out of the oven. Mama took off her apron and got her purse. "I'm going to the beauty parlor before I go shopping." "You're taking her, aren't you?" Calvin asked, pointing at his sister. "Too hot to be dragging a little child around," Mama told him. "You and Rodney can look after her."

She gave Trudy a kiss and then fixed her son with a serious look. "You be nice. None of your tricks, understand?"

"Let me in!" Trudy cried, banging on Calvin's bedroom door. "I told you, bug off!" Calvin said from inside. "We're making something."
"I could help," Trudy said, not loud enough for anyone to hear. The door opened. "Hey," Calvin asked her, "want to be in an experiment?"

Inside Calvin's room, Rodney was working on a contraption made out of erector set parts. It had a small motor that turned a cardboard disc with a black and white spiral painted on it. "Okay," said Calvin, "sit right here and look at this thing." Rodney hooked up a battery to the motor and the disc began to spin.

Trudy squirmed around, but then sat perfectly still, glassy-eyed, staring straight at the disc. Calvin waved his hand in front of her. She didn't even blink. "That's creepy," Rodney said. "She looks like some kind of statue."

Calvin leaned close to his sister. "Trudy," he asked, "can you hear me?" She nodded slowly. "Trudy, you aren't a little girl—you are a . . ." He stopped and thought for a moment. "You are a dog." Calvin snapped his fingers. Trudy rolled off the chair and onto the floor, standing on her hands and knees, with her tongue hanging out. "Trudy?" Calvin asked. His sister looked at him and barked. "Cripes," shouted Rodney. "It worked!"

"Let's take her outside," Calvin said. "C'mon, girl!" He patted his leg. Trudy followed the boys to the top of the stairs, then stopped and made a whining noise. "My cousin has a puppy like that," Rodney explained. "You need to help her down." Calvin picked his sister up.

In the backyard, he set her on the grass. Rodney tossed a stick and Trudy shot after it on all fours. Then she spotted a squirrel and started barking. "She sure is loud for being so small," said Rodney. Mrs. Bemis, the old lady who lived behind Calvin, thought so, too.

Her eyesight was pretty poor, but her hearing was fine. She leaned out her window and told the boys to take their noisy dog inside or she'd get the dogcatcher after him. Calvin called his sister, who trotted over to him. Mrs. Bemis squinted at Trudy. "What sort of dog is that, anyway?"

"She's a mutt," Rodney said. "Well, keep it inside," Mrs. Bemis told the boys, and slammed her window shut. Calvin gave his friend a dirty look. "Don't call my sister a mutt." "Sorry," said Rodney. "It's not like she'll remember. She won't know what happened after you snap her out of it."

Calvin looked at Trudy, with her tongue hanging out, panting and drooling. She was starting to make him feel weird. He knelt beside her. "Trudy, can you hear me?" She looked at him and licked his face. "Yuck," said Rodney.

Calvin wiped his cheek. "Now listen," he told his sister, "when I snap my fingers, you are going to be a little girl again. Okay?" Calvin stood up and snapped his fingers, but Trudy stayed on her hands and knees. Another squirrel ran across the yard and Trudy chased it, howling like a hound.

Calvin ran after her, snapping his fingers, but his sister wouldn't stop barking. Mrs. Bemis threw open her window. "What did I tell you boys!" she yelled. Rodney and Calvin grabbed Trudy and carried her back inside.

In the kitchen, Trudy looked at her brother, still with her tongue out and panting. "She must be thirsty," said Rodney, who got a bowl of water. Calvin pleaded with his sister to wake up, but she wouldn't stop slurping water from the bowl on the floor. "Say that word," Rodney told him, "you know, what Lomax said—Boboditi, Momojiti. Something like that." "Rootabidi," Calvin said. "The word was Rootabidi." They both yelled at Trudy, "ROOTABIDI!" and snapped their fingers, but nothing happened.

"You sure that's the word?" Rodney asked. Calvin wasn't sure. What he did know, for certain, was that he was going to be in big trouble when Mama came home and saw Trudy trying to scratch her ear with her foot and barking at squirrels.

"I've got an idea," Rodney said. "We can take her to Lomax. He knows what to say. He'll fix her." Calvin agreed. They could take Trudy to the bus stop, go to the theater, and find the magician.

"Hey, Trudy," Calvin said, "want to go for a walk?" She looked up, trotted to the back door, and started scratching it, then let out a howl.

"You know," said Rodney, "you can't take dogs on the bus." "She's not a dog," Calvin answered. "Well," Rodney told him, "when she starts sniffing people and barking, you're going to wish she was." Rodney was right. The bus might be a problem, so Calvin got his old wagon out from the garage.

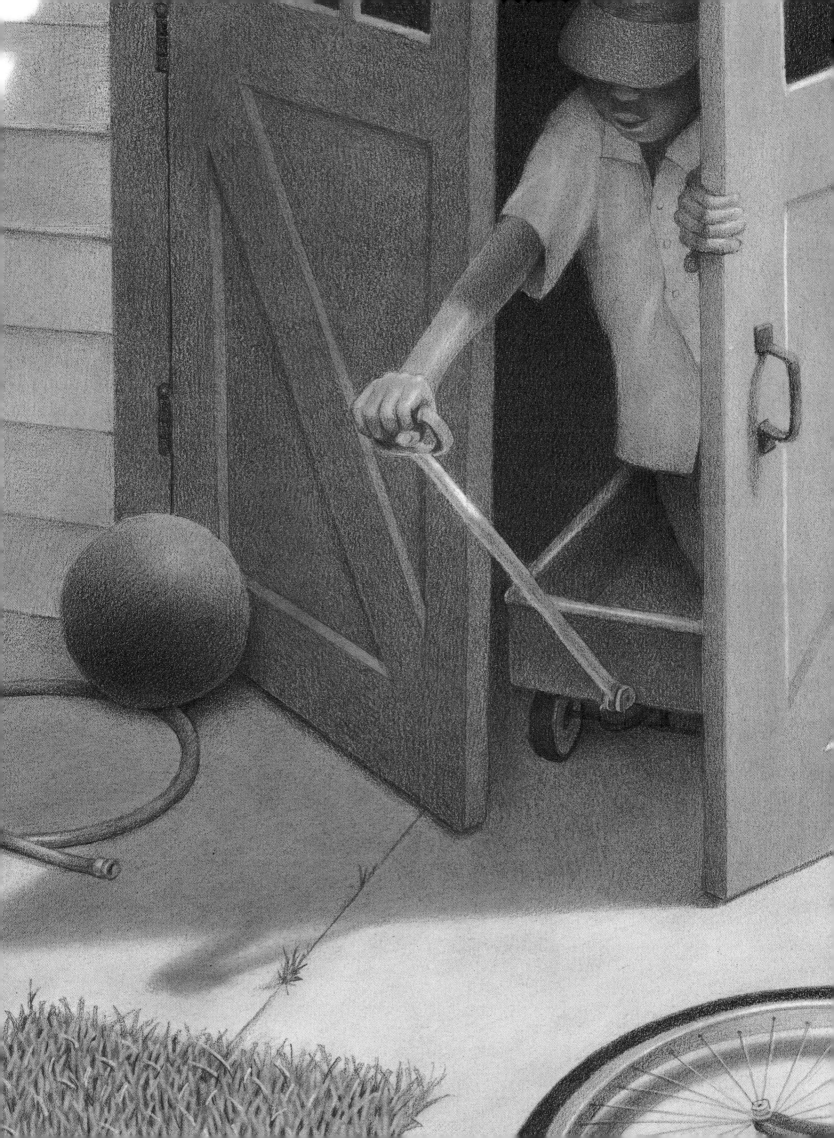

It would be a long trip on a very hot day, but Calvin knew that if his little sister was going to stop barking and start walking on two feet, he had to get her to the magician. So they put Trudy in the wagon and started pulling.

The boys were sweating and breathing hard, but the theater was only two blocks away when they reached the top of the hill on High Street. An ice cream parlor stood on the corner, so they searched their pockets and found enough change for one cone. Rodney went inside and came out with a frosty dip of chocolate chip. He took a lick and passed it to his friend.

Trudy looked at Calvin, panting. He held out the cone to his sister. "Careful," Rodney warned, but it was too late. Trudy took three quick bites. "That's how puppies eat," Rodney told Calvin, who was staring at the empty cone.

Rodney grabbed his arm. "Look, look, it's him!" A big black limousine rolled past the boys, stopping at a traffic light. In the back seat sat the magician. "Mr. Lomax! Mr. Lomax!" Calvin called out. The light changed. Calvin ran into the street, waving his arms, but the car pulled away. He walked back to the wagon. There was nothing left to do now but go home.

"Is she sleeping?" Calvin asked. He and Rodney had pulled Trudy almost half the way back. "Guess so," said Rodney, looking at the little girl curled up in the wagon. "Hey," said Calvin, "I bet when she wakes up, she won't be a dog anymore." He poked his sister in the shoulder. She snarled and tried to bite him. "Jeez," said Rodney. "Never bother puppies when they're sleeping—don't you know that?"

Trudy laid her head back down and closed her eyes. Calvin was so tired that he wished he could, too, but he and Rodney took hold of the wagon handle and kept on pulling, block after block, under the hot afternoon sun.

Mama's car was not there when the boys finally rolled the wagon up Calvin's driveway, but they knew she would be home soon. Trudy was still asleep. Rodney whispered, "I've got an idea." He led Calvin away from the wagon. "What we need to do is really surprise her, like when you scare the hiccups out of somebody. Know what I mean?"

In the garage, the boys found a bucket and a couple of trash can lids. Calvin filled the bucket with water, and the boys tiptoed up to Trudy. Rodney banged the lids together and Calvin dumped the bucket of water onto his sister. She screamed and jumped to her feet. "It worked!" Rodney yelled, and at that very moment, Mama pulled into the driveway.

Trudy started to cry. Mama climbed out of the car with a look on her face that Calvin could not remember ever having seen before. "Uh-oh," Rodney said. He put the trash can lids down. "See you later," he told Calvin, and lit out for his house.

Mama marched up the driveway. Trudy stood in the wagon, sopping wet and crying her eyes out. While Calvin was wondering if he should explain that he had turned Trudy into a dog, but that she was okay now, Mama lifted her daughter from the wagon. Then she grabbed Calvin by his shirt collar and hauled him into the house.

Calvin had smelled the spaghetti sauce cooking downstairs earlier, but he was still shut in his room when the sun went down. He was wondering if he'd be getting his birthday meal when Trudy knocked on the door. She held a tray with his dinner on it: a peanut butter sandwich, a pickle, and a glass of milk.

She set the tray on Calvin's desk, next to the contraption with the spiral disc. "What's that for?" she asked.

"For hypnotizing. I used it on you," he told her. "Me?" Trudy said. "Yep," answered Calvin, "I turned you into a dog." He started chuckling. "Had you running around on your hand and knees, barking and drooling."

Trudy waited for her brother to stop laughing and then asked him, "How come I don't remember?" " 'Cause that's how it works," Calvin told her. "If you did, that'd mean you weren't hypnotized."

"Oh," said Trudy. She watched her brother chew unhappily on his peanut butter sandwich. "The spaghetti was really good," she told him. "So was the cake." Calvin just grunted. "Know what else I liked?" Trudy asked. "That ice cream I had this afternoon. Chocolate chip's my favorite."